THE
SIR HERBER[T]

By Kate McMullan
Illustrated by Bill Basso

GROSSET & DUNLAP • NEW YORK

For Aaron, Alec, Alexander, Daniel, David,
Dominique, Eleanor, Emma, Henry, James,
Jamie, Joachim, Journey, Julia, Kaya, Reece, River,
Sage, their wonderful teacher, Anne Bukowsky,
and especially for Henry who said,
"dragon ghost"—K. McM.

Text copyright © 2004 by Kate McMullan. Illustrations copyright © 2004 by Bill Basso. All rights reserved. Published by Grosset & Dunlap, a division of Penguin Young Readers Group, 345 Hudson Street, New York, New York 10014. DRAGON SLAYERS' ACADEMY and GROSSET & DUNLAP are trademarks of Penguin Group (USA) Inc. Printed in the U.S.A.

Library of Congress Cataloging-in-Publication Data

McMullan, Kate.
  The ghost of Sir Herbert Dungeonstone / by Kate McMullan ; illustrated by Bill Basso.
    p. cm. — (Dragon Slayers' Academy ; 12)
  Summary: While Headmaster Mordred is trying to impress a new student, who he believes to be the first female at Dragon Slayers' Academy, the ghost of one of the school's founders besieges the halls seeking his stolen gold.
  ISBN 0-448-43530-6 (pbk.)
  [1. Ghosts—Fiction. 2. Knights and knighthood—Fiction. 3. Sex role—Fiction. 4. Schools—Fiction.] I. Basso, Bill, ill. II. Title.
  PZ7.M2295Gh 2004
  [Fic]—dc22   2004007986

ISBN 0-448-43530-6   10 9 8 7 6 5 4

Chapter I

"Ready, Wiglaf?" Erica called from the far end of the Class I dorm. "Step on it, Angus," she added. "We do not want to be late for the feast."

"There won't be any feast," Angus said as he pulled on a semi-clean DSA tunic. "Uncle Mordred will give us the same supper as always—eel casserole and lumpen pudding."

No doubt Angus was right, Wiglaf thought as he stepped into his breeches. But he didn't mind. His mother's cooking back home was much, much worse.

Angus went on. "I wonder what's happened to the latest goodie box Mother sent. It should have come."

Erica hurried over to the boys. "Are my

braids sticking out from my helmet?" she whispered, turning around.

Wiglaf checked. "No," he told her. "No one would ever guess you are a girl."

"Shhh!" Erica looked around to make sure no one had heard. "Do not say that! Mordred will kick me out of DSA if he finds out."

"Your secret is safe with us," Wiglaf said.

Angus nodded. "My lips are sealed."

Erica sighed as she buckled her tool belt. "I do get tired of being the only girl at DSA. And of wearing this disguise."

Wiglaf pulled his helmet over his carrot-colored hair. He followed his friends out of the dorm and down the wide staircase.

"Was not that moaning last night awful?" Erica said as they went.

"Moaning?" Angus asked. "I heard nothing."

"Nor did I," Wiglaf added.

"Really?" said Erica. "Oh, it was terrible. I hardly slept a wink." They reached the first floor and headed for the dining hall. "I have very sensitive hearing. Sir Lancelot is the same way. In his book, *A Knight Like I*, he tells how he can hear even the faintest sound."

Angus rolled his eyes. But Wiglaf smiled. He knew that Erica's fondest wish was to be a noble knight just like Sir Lancelot.

The three walked under a wide stone arch into the crowded DSA dining hall.

In the glimmering flames from wall-mounted torches, Wiglaf spotted the big Marley brothers—Barley, Charlie, Farley, and Harley. They were bigger and taller than any of the DSA teachers. At another table nearby, Wiglaf saw Coach Plungett, the slaying teacher. And the weapons teacher, Master X. He was an ex-executioner who still wore a black hood over his head. He saw Brother Dave, the DSA librarian. And Mordred's sister, Lady Lobelia. She wore a purple gown trimmed in feathered plumes.

Wiglaf also spied three big-boned, yellow-haired strangers sitting at the head table. A father, mother, and daughter. The father had many gold chains around his neck. The mother sported a necklace with a huge blue stone. The girl wore pearls and a fancy gown.

The girl was also chomping on a bright green wad of what could only be Smilin' Hal's Tree Sap Chewing Gum. Wiglaf quickly looked around for Mordred. He always sent gum chewers straight to the dungeon for a time-out.

"Who are they?" Wiglaf asked Angus.

Angus shrugged. "They look rich."

"Hey!" said Erica, pointing. "Look at that!"

A black cloth was draped over the arch at the back of the room. It hid words carved into stone that said DRAGON SLAYERS' ACADEMY FOR LADS.

"All stand for the headmaster!" called Yorick, Mordred's scout. "All stand!"

Everyone rose. Mordred strode to the head

table where the three guests were seated. He was decked out in a rich purple velvet robe with gold trim. And a matching hat with a golden tassel.

Mordred smiled. His gold tooth gleamed in the torchlight. His violet eyes shone.

"Greetings!" he boomed. "Tomorrow is Founders Day. And tonight we feast to honor the school founders...and to welcome a new student. A student who brings a big change to DSA!"

"When I came here," Wiglaf whispered to Angus, "there was no feast in my honor. My first night at DSA, I washed a mountain of dirty dishes!"

"But I get ahead of myself," Mordred said. "First, let us hear the heartwarming story of DSA's founding. Students with poems?"

Wiglaf, Angus, and Erica jumped up. So did Baldrick. Torblad came, too, carrying his trumpet.

"Many years ago," Mordred began, "inside the Dark Forest's deepest cave lived the two meanest dragons in the world. On top of the Dark Forest's highest hill lived the two meanest robbers in the world. Any wayfarer who wandered into the Dark Forest with a bag of gold wandered out empty-handed—if he was lucky enough to escape the fire-breathing dragons. Then one day, into the Dark Forest rode two bold knights."

Torblad put his trumpet to his lips and blew: TOOT TOOTY TOOT TOOT!!

Erica stepped forward and, in a confident voice, began to read:

> *"I am Sir Herbert Dungeonstone!*
> *For doing great good deeds I'm known.*
> *I slew two dragons in their cave.*
> *They never more will flame or rave*
> *Or bar-b-que poor passersby.*
> *Oh, brave Sir Dungeonstone am I!"*

Erica stepped back. Angus cleared his throat.

"I am Sir Ichabod Popquiz,
And slaying robbers is my biz.
I snuck up on their hilltop lair,
And drew my sword and slew the pair!
I ran them through; that's not so odd
For me, the brave Sir Ichabod!"

Now it was Wiglaf's turn. His hands were shaking as he held the piece of parchment.

"The robbers' lair was filled with loot,
Not that the good knights gave a hoot.
They didn't care for treasure much,
For gold or gems or coins and such.
Still, it seemed unwise, unfair,
To leave the loot just lying there.
Sir Herbert said, 'With just one jewel,
We might be bold and start a school!'
'Oh, let's!' Sir Ichabod did say.
'We'll teach young lads the proper way

To slay vile dragons in their caves,
And set upon Dark Forest knaves!' "

Torblad blew another blast on his trumpet:
TOOT TOOTY TOOT TOOT!

Baldrick stepped up. He wiped his runny nose on his sleeve and read:

"That's how our fair school came to be:
Dragon Slayers' Academy!"

"Bravo!" cried Lady Lobelia, jumping up.

The yellow-haired daughter took out her gum and gave a loud whistle. TWEEEEEEET!

"All right!" she called. "So, Mordred—when do we eat around here?"

Chapter 2

The dining hall grew still. Wiglaf froze. Students didn't call the DSA headmaster *Mordred*. They called him *sir*! Would he send the girl to the dungeon...or worse?

But Mordred only smiled. "Soon, my dear," he said, "very soon. But first, Coach Plungett! Master X! Forward please!"

The teachers began pushing two gleaming giant-sized statues of noble knights toward the head table.

"Our founders!" cried Mordred. "The old statues of them were...lost in a terrible accident." Mordred pretended to wipe a tear from his eye. "Now, here are brand-new statues of our noble founders, Sir Herbert

Dungeonstone and Sir Ichabod Popquiz!"

"Oh, puh-lease!" whispered Angus. "Like we don't know the old statues were made of soap and got used up last Bath Day!"

Wiglaf nodded. There was no mistaking Sir Herbert Dungeonstone, he thought, with his eye patch and his little, thin mustache.

As the clapping died down, Erica raised her hand. Mordred motioned for her to put it down. If there was one thing he disliked, it was a student who asked questions. But Erica thought he had called on her.

"Sir?" she said. "What happened to our noble founders *after* they founded DSA?"

Mordred glared at Erica. "Ah, well, er—in time, Sir Herbert and Sir Ichabod grew too old to run DSA. They talked to thousands of worthy candidates. And they picked *me* to take over their good work. They retired to the Home for Aged Knights on a palm-tree covered island off the coast of Greece. They are very, very happy." He smiled.

SNAP! The yellow-haired girl snapped her gum.

Once more, the room quieted.

Students held their breath. Surely now Mordred would send her to the dungeon.

But the DSA headmaster only chuckled. He glanced fondly at the girl and said, "Time to reveal my big surprise!"

Torblad stood and trumpeted once more: TOOT TOOTY TOOT TOOT!

Master X and Coach Plungett yanked the cloth off the stone archway. It fell away and revealed a brand-new sign: DRAGON SLAYERS' ACADEMY FOR LADS AND LASS.

Erica gasped. "He knows I am a lass!"

"And he is not kicking you out of school!" said Wiglaf happily.

Erica rose to her feet. "Thank you, sir!" she cried. "This is a happy day, indeed!"

"Sit down!" Mordred bellowed. "I'll tell you when to stand up! I'll tell you when a day is happy! SIT!"

Erica quickly sat. She looked stunned. Every month, she won the Future Dragon Slayer of the Month Award. She was not used to being treated this way.

Mordred beamed adoringly at the yellow-haired family.

"Let me introduce Lord and Lady Smotherbottom," he said.

The big-boned couple stood. They smiled toothy smiles and waved.

"And," Mordred went on, "their very lovely, athletic, talented daughter, Janice."

The girl stood. Wiglaf saw that she was as tall as Harley Marley.

"Hi ya, lads," said Janice, chewing boldly.

"Janice Smotherbottom," Mordred went on, "is the very first student in the long history of Dragon Slayers' Academy to pay her tuition in solid gold coins—up front!" His violet eyes spun with joy.

"Uh, sir?" Coach Plungett elbowed the spellbound headmaster. "I think you mean to say that Janice is our first..."

"Our first *girl*!" cried Mordred. "Yes! Girl! Yes! That's what I meant to say. Our first lass! Female! Little woman!"

Erica's mouth dropped open in surprise.

"Oh, Mordie!" cried Lady Lobelia. "This *is* a bold step!"

"Janice is going to stay with us for a couple of days," Mordred added, "to see if she likes it here. I want all you lads to make our one-and-only lass feel welcome!"

Chapter 3

"One-and-only lass, my foot!" grumbled Erica. She, Angus, and Wiglaf made their tired way up the wide stone steps to the dorm room.

A feast had indeed been served—to those at the head table. The students got the usual eel casserole. Afterward, the three friends had been tapped by Frypot, the cook, for cleanup duty.

"I was the first girl at DSA," Erica went on. "Not Janice What's-her-bottom!"

"Your parents are king and queen of the realm," said Wiglaf. "They must have paid your tuition up front in gold."

"No," said Erica. "The truly rich never pay up front."

They walked into the Class I dorm and stopped short.

"What *happened?*" cried Wiglaf.

"Keep it down!" Torblad called. "We're trying to sleep."

Even in the dim glow of the lone night-light torch, they saw that all the cots had been shoved over to one side. A brown curtain had been strung across the center of the room. A hastily made sign tacked onto the curtain said: CLASS I LASS'S DORM.

Erica strode over to the curtain and swept it aside. For the second time that evening, she gasped.

Wiglaf and Angus ran over to her. When they saw what was behind the curtain, they were stunned.

A big gold canopy bed stood against the wall. A matching wardrobe, chest of drawers, and dressing table surrounded it. A jousting pole and a pair of crossed lances hung over the bed.

A loud snap sounded. The gum-chewing Janice rose from a trunk she was unpacking.

"Hi ya, lads," she said. "I'm all moved in."

Everything about Janice was big, Wiglaf thought. Her cheeks were dotted with big freckles. She had a big space between her two front teeth. She had big, broad shoulders.

"Hello," said Angus. "I'm Angus."

Wiglaf told her his name, too.

"I'm, uh, Eric," said Erica.

"Well, you know who I am," said Janice.

"What school did you come from?" asked Angus.

"Dragon Whackers." SNAP!!

"How come you changed schools?" asked Wiglaf.

"Mordred showed up at Whackers one day and saw me win a jousting match," Janice replied. "He said he wanted me for the DSA jousting team, and Mom and Dad said I could transfer."

Wiglaf shot Angus and Erica a look. DSA didn't have any jousting team.

Janice yawned and stretched. "Listen, lads, I'm beat," she said. "My Whackers pals threw lots of farewell parties. I haven't slept in a week." She took the wad of green gum from her mouth and stuck it on top of a bedpost. "Nighty-night!"

As they turned to go, Erica caught sight of the Sir Lancelot tapestry that had hung on the wall over her cot. It lay crumpled on the floor. Erica darted over and picked up the stitched portrait of her beloved knight, then hurried after Wiglaf and Angus.

Brrrr! Wiglaf slipped under his covers fully dressed.

"Good night," he whispered.

"Night," murmured Angus.

"How can you sleep?" hissed Erica. "It's not fair! *I* am the first DSA lass ever. And I am a princess! But did I ask for a bigger share of the dorm room? I did not."

"Uh-uh," Wiglaf managed sleepily.

"Jousting team, indeed!" Erica muttered. Then she was still for a moment. "Surely you hear it now!"

Wiglaf had begun to drift off to sleep. "Wha—?"

"Don't you hear it?" Erica whispered.

"Hear what?" said Wiglaf.

"The awful moaning!" cried Erica. "It is coming from deep inside this very castle!"

Chapter 4

"Come!" Erica shook Angus and Wiglaf until they rolled out of their cots. "We must find out what is making that awful sound!"

Wiglaf pulled himself to his feet. He listened but heard nothing.

Angus groaned. "I don't hear anything."

"You think I'm making it up?" said Erica. "I'm not!" She put her hands over her ears. "Ohhh! It is a terrible sound! I'm going down there, and you're both coming with me. Get your swords. Let us be on our way!"

Without giving Wiglaf and Angus a chance to say no, Erica dragged her friends down the wide stone steps. She lit the way with her mini-torch. At the bottom, she stopped and tilted her head. "The moaning is coming from the dungeon."

Wiglaf's heart began to race. The dungeon was scary enough during the daytime. But at night? He didn't want to *think* about how scary it would be. With a last glance through a slit in the castle wall at the full, silvery moon, he followed Erica and Angus down to the dungeon.

Erica opened the door.

Wiglaf felt for the hilt of his sword. His heart beat like a drum.

Erica stepped into the pitch-dark dungeon. She shone her torch around. "Empty," she declared.

Wiglaf sighed. "Oh, good!"

Erica frowned. "The moans are coming from below," she said. "How can that be?"

Angus swallowed. "I happen to know that there is a Deeper Dungeon beneath this one."

"Then lead the way," Erica commanded.

Angus's hand trembled as he took the mini-torch from Erica. He led them to a hidden staircase. Down, down, down they crept. The air grew thin. The smell of mold grew thick.

Wiglaf heard a faint, high-pitched wail.

"I hear it!" he whispered. "I do! 'Tis awful!"

"I told you," said Erica.

At the bottom of the stairway, Angus stopped. Without a word, the three joined hands. They inched forward together.

The mini-torch barely lit the darkness. Wiglaf heard the moaning plainly now. The back of his neck tingled. What *was* it?

Angus stopped before an old wooden door. "This is it," he whispered.

Erica snatched the torch. She drew her sword. "Open the door, Wiglaf."

Wiglaf's hand was none too steady as he reached for the cold circle of iron. He pulled. The door creaked open. A sickening smell of something old, something rotten whooshed out.

"Yikes!" Wiglaf cried as bats darted out of the Deeper Dungeon.

Ducking to avoid the flapping wings, Erica stepped into the Deeper Dungeon. She waved her torch from side to side. "Empty!" She whirled around. "Angus, what now?"

"Please!" cried Angus. "Let us go back to bed!"

"Yes, let's!" whispered Wiglaf.

But Erica only glared at Angus. "Tell me!"

"Th-th-there is the Deepest Dungeon," Angus croaked. "That is where the Duke of Doublechin was tortured. The poor man was tickled for a solid month without stopping! Oh, the Deepest Dungeon is a bad place! No one goes there! Ever!"

"Is that so?" said Erica. "Well, we are. Now!"

Wiglaf trembled as Angus led them down a dark passageway to another staircase. This one was so narrow that clammy stone walls pressed into them as they went. The stairs were steep, moss-covered, and slippery. Wiglaf nearly choked on the strong, fishy odor.

One last step, and Wiglaf found himself ankle-deep in something wet.

"Gack!" cried Angus. "This is disgusting!"

"It is only moat water," said Erica. She shone her torch downward.

Wiglaf's stomach gave a sickening lurch. "Oh, no!" he cried. "We're standing in rotten eel guts and bubbling moat slime!"

"Forward!" growled Erica.

On they waded. As they neared the Deepest Dungeon, the moaning and wailing grew louder still. If Wiglaf had not been wearing his helmet, his hair would have been standing on end.

At last they came to an ancient iron door. Erica shone her torch upon it. It was coated in thick, slimy, green moss.

Suddenly, the door began to open by itself.

The three jumped back.

Wiglaf could not breathe.

In the mossy, green doorway stood a knight! A knight with a patch over one eye and a wispy mustache. A knight wearing silver armor. A knight glowing with an eerie white light. A knight waving a chain-mailed hand, inviting them to come into the Deepest Dungeon.

"Hello, sir!" cried Erica eagerly. She started forward.

"Wait!" Wiglaf cried. Something was wrong with the knight. But what?

Erica paid no attention to Wiglaf.

"Greetings, knight!" she said.

Now Wiglaf saw what was wrong. He could see right through the knight! He could see all the way to the back wall of the Deepest Dungeon.

Wiglaf grabbed Erica's arm. "Stop!" he cried. "It's a ghost!"

Chapter 5

"AAAAAAAAAAA!" screamed Angus, Wiglaf, and even Erica.

They whirled around, stumbling through the muck, fleeing the Deepest Dungeon.

The ghost appeared suddenly before them.

Wiglaf skidded to a stop. Angus and then Erica slammed into him from behind. The three clutched one another.

"Tell old Herbie where the gold is hidden," growled the ghost.

"We know nothing of any gold," said Erica.

"Please!" cried Angus. "Let us go!"

The ghost laughed and said, "Let's have a little heart-to-heart."

They waded back to the Deepest Dungeon,

the ghost prodding them with an icy finger.

Once inside, the ghost turned over an iron bench and ordered, "Sit!"

Wiglaf sat. Oooh, that bench was freezing! He thought his bum might turn to ice.

The ghost dragged over a big iron chair. It had spikes all over the seat and the back. As the ghost sat down, the spikes slid right through his transparent armor.

A mug sat on the floor beside the ghost. Steam rose from it. The ghost picked up the mug and took a long gulp. Wiglaf was horrified to see bright red liquid flow down his ghostly throat all the way to his stomach.

Wiglaf thought there was something familiar about the ghost.

"H-have we met you before, sir?" he asked.

The ghost ignored him, taking another swig of the red brew. "Think hard, me little friends," he said. "You must have seen that headmaster of yours sneaking around, trying to find a spot to hide his gold."

"No, sir," said Erica. "We haven't."

"I know who you are!" cried Wiglaf suddenly. "Sir Herbert Dungeonstone!"

"Bingo!" The ghost grinned.

"Oh, sir!" said Erica. "I had the honor of reading a poem about you this very evening. Is good Sir Ichabod here with you?"

"Nah," said Sir Herbert. "It's only me. Icky's resting peaceful in his grave, like I wants to do." He frowned. "It isn't because Icky has a clear conscience. Not after all the blokes he robbed!"

Sir Ichabod? A robber? Wiglaf was confused. What was the ghost saying?

"But I have to say this for Icky," Sir Herbert went on. "He was never greedy. Took up robbing for the sport of it, Icky did. Had no real love for the loot. But me?" The ghost chuckled. "I took up robbing for the gold. Ah, how I loves me gold!"

All this talk of gold reminded Wiglaf of

Mordred. He loved gold, too.

"I never got enough of it to suit me," Sir Herbert went on. "No matter how high me stack of coins grew, I always hoped it would grow higher. I was greedy. Still am. And I cannot rest in my grave until I get me gold."

"Hold it," said Angus. "Are you saying that you and Sir Ichabod were robbers?"

"That's right." The ghost nodded.

"No!" cried Erica. "That cannot be!"

"Do you doubt me?" Sir Herbert smirked. "Can't say I blame you. I lie as easy as I steal. Still, I happen to be telling the truth."

"Sir! I am the only student ever to check out *The History of Dragon Slayers' Academy* from the library," said Erica. "I read it cover to cover. You and Sir Ichabod were noble knights!"

"Nah. Your headmaster has been feeding you a great heap of beans," said the ghost. "Listen up, me little friends, and I shall tell you the real history of Dragon Slayers' Academy."

Chapter 6

Wiglaf shifted on the ice-cold bench as he listened to the ghost begin his tale.

"In life, I, Herbert Dungeonstone, was a knave," said the ghost. "I was a highwayman, purse-snatcher, robber. Me partner-in-crime was Ichabod Popquiz. We dressed as knights so folks trusted us. Pretty clever, eh? We robbed everyone—lords, ladies, friars, pilgrims, farmers. We flipped many a poor peasant upside down and shook his only penny out of his pocket. We robbed little children's lunch money."

"You *were* a lowly knave!" cried Erica.

"The lowest." The ghost smiled. "One summer's day, some thirty years back, me and

Icky decides it's time to move from our hilltop hideout to our cave hideout on the far side of the Dark Forest. So we puts on our great coats, which are made special-like, with dozens of pockets inside the lining. Me and Icky stuffs every last bit of our gold into those pockets."

"Wasn't it awfully heavy?" said Angus.

"Gold is never too heavy for the greedy," said Sir Herbert. "Off we goes, me and Icky. On our way, we pass Smilin' Hal's Eatery and decide to have us a nice lunch. After we eats, we robs old Hal of every last cent in his till. We walks on then and who should come along but Mordred de Marvelous."

"You knew my uncle Mordred?" asked Angus.

"You're related?" The ghost rubbed his hands together. "Ah, that could be helpful." He took another drink of the steaming brew. "Everybody knew Mordie back then," he went on. "He was a wrestler. Big and strong as an ox.

Smelled like an ox, too, as I remember. Me and Icky used to bet on Mordie's matches. Always won good money." He smiled, remembering.

"Go on," said Angus.

"Mordie falls in walking with us," said the ghost. "He asks our names, and we tell him— adding 'sir' for good measure. Hearing we was knights, Mordie brightens. Says how he is starting a school for lads. He has its name all picked out: Dragon Slayers' Academy."

"Is this true?" asked Wiglaf.

The ghost reached out a cold hand and grabbed Wiglaf's wrist. " 'Tis!" he cried.

"Mordie tells us his plan: His lads shall slay dragons and bring him their golden hoards." The ghost winked his good eye. "Me and Icky had him totally fooled, so he asks us, how about investing in his school? We say maybe, going along with him. All the while, we is eyeing the little pouch hanging from his belt. It was filled with gold. I could smell it."

Wiglaf's eyes grew wide. "Did you rob Mordred?"

"Not exactly," said the ghost. "On we walks until we comes to a lonely spot in the Dark Forest. No one around. No one to hear screams. Old Icky gives me the nod. And we sets upon Mordie, trying to snatch his pouch. But when it comes to saving his gold, Mordie is too fast for us. And too big. He picks us up by the scruffs of our necks and dangles us in front of him like a pair of kittens."

"Just what you deserved," said Angus.

"Right away we sees we have made a bad mistake," said the ghost. "We begs for mercy. But Mordie's violet eyes light up, and he says that me and Icky is about to invest in his school. We say, yes, fine. We was in no position to argue. Then Mordie, who knows a thing or two about inside pockets, has us open up our coats and he takes every last golden coin. We wuz robbed!"

Herbert Dungeonstone let out a terrible moan. Wiglaf shuddered.

"Mordie ties us to a nearby tree," the ghost went on at last. "He says he has a fine way to repay us."

"I knew he was honest!" said Erica.

"Honest? Hah!" Herbert Dungeonstone snorted. "Mordie says Sir Herbert Dungeonstone and Sir Ichabod Popquiz will ever forth be honored as the true and noble founders of DSA."

The ghost put the red brew to his lips and drained the mug dry. He pounded his chest and belched up a small red-tinted cloud. Then his lips curved into a snarl.

"Me and Icky was robbed by your head-master!" the ghost howled. "Robbed! Now me ghost can't rest, thinking of it. That's why I've come—to get me gold so that I can lie easy in my grave. I'm going to search this old castle from its soggy bottom to its tippy-top tower until I find it."

"What...what happens if...you don't find it?" asked Angus, his voice shaking.

"If I don't find me gold," said the ghost, "all that will be left of Dragon Slayers' Academy is a great heap of rubble!"

Chapter 7

"Sir! No!" cried Wiglaf. "Please! Do not wreck Dragon Slayers' Academy."

"Then," said the greedy ghost, "help me get me hands on me gold."

Now Angus spoke up. "My uncle Mordred once kept piles of gold in his safe."

"I knew it!" The ghost leaned forward in his spiky chair. "Get the safe open, lad. I'll take the gold and be gone."

"Alas," said Angus. "The gold is spent. School Inspectors came last spring. They said Uncle Mordred had to make improvements, or they would close him down. Fixing this old castle took every bit of his gold."

"Not *his* gold!" cried the ghost. "It's *me own*

precious gold!"

The ghost floated up off his spiky chair. He grabbed a pair of leg irons and ripped them from the wall. He tore down a torch holder.

"See?" he cried. "I meant what I said."

"But we do not know where any gold is!" cried Wiglaf. "Honest!"

The ghost grabbed the iron slab that passed for a bed in the Deepest Dungeon, yanked it from its moorings, and flung it to the floor.

The three pupils looked on, horrified, as the ghost picked up the spiky chair and hurled it down, breaking off its legs.

Erica leaned toward Wiglaf and Angus. "Mordred has that bag of gold from the Smotherbottoms, remember?" she whispered.

Herbert Dungeonstone's ghost shrieked, "I heard that! Did Mordie rob these Smotherbottoms, too?"

"No," said Angus. "They paid him tuition for their daughter. We can ask Mordred to give you some of that gold."

"Not some!" said the ghost. "ALL! When you are greedy, some is never enough. Why, all is hardly enough."

"If Mordred gives you all the gold, will you go away?" asked Wiglaf.

"I give you me word." The ghost ripped a pair of wrist irons from the wall. "The sooner you get me that gold, the sooner I'll be gone!"

Then—poof! Herbert Dungeonstone disappeared. So did his ghostly glow.

In the dark, Erica fumbled for her mini-torch. She flicked it on.

"Hey!" she yelped. "My sword!"

Erica's sword leaped out of its scabbard, flipped, and began slashing at the three.

"Egad!" cried Angus. He hit the floor.

"Stop!" cried Erica. "Give that back!"

The only answer was another slash.

"Angus! Wiglaf!" cried Erica. "Run!"

They sloshed through the slimy muck. The

sword swooshed behind them. It poked Wiglaf's backside. Ouch!

The three raced up the narrow stairway and past the Deeper Dungeon.

"Call me name when you've got the gold!" cried the invisible ghost. "Until then, I'll be wrecking the place!"

Then—CRASH! BANG!—a suit of armor in the passageway toppled to the floor.

"He means it!" cried Wiglaf as they sped up another stairway.

"Angus, wake Mordred," said Erica as they ran.

"Me?" cried Angus. "Why me?"

"He is your uncle," said Erica.

"Wiglaf, you wake him," puffed Angus, very much out of breath as they reached the ground floor of DSA.

Wiglaf swallowed. Mordred disliked students who woke him up even more than he disliked students who asked questions.

But he needn't have worried. As they ran, the headmaster's door flew open, and out came Mordred. He wore a nightshirt and sleeping cap. His feet were bare. In one hand, he held a torch. Wiglaf was surprised to see that tucked under his other arm was a large, brown teddy bear.

"I should have known you three were making this racket!" Mordred yelled.

BOOM! BANG! The castle floor shook.

"Zounds!" exclaimed Mordred. "Stop it!"

"It's not us, sir!" said Erica.

BAM! BAM! BAM!

"Stop, I say!" cried Mordred. "You'll wake up Janice! If she doesn't like it here, she'll leave! Then her mum and dad will want their gold back." His violet eyes spun at the awful thought.

Wiglaf glanced up at the landing at the top of the wide stone staircase. There stood Janice! She had a sleep mask pushed up on top of her messy yellow hair. Her eyes were only half open. In one hand, she held a long lance. She looked grumpy as she slowly chewed her gum.

"Hey, Mordred!" she shouted. "What's going on down there?"

"Go back to beddie-bye, Janice, my dear!" called Mordred. "We're just planning a little Founders Day fun!"

Chapter 8

Janice frowned and vanished from the railing.

"Egad!" cried Mordred, hugging his teddy bear tightly. "What if Janice isn't happy? Wait'll I catch the scoundrel who woke her up. I'll toss him into the dungeon for a year!"

"Uncle!" said Angus. "It is no scoundrel. It is Sir Herbert Dungeonstone."

"Only he is not really a sir," added Erica.

"But he *is* really a ghost," said Wiglaf. "And he has come to get...something he believes belongs to him."

Mordred narrowed his eyes suspiciously.

"You little varlets!" he roared. "You've tapped my cider keg, haven't you?"

"Never, sir!" said Erica. "This is the truth. In the Deepest Dungeon, we found the ghost of Herbert Dungeonstone. And unless you give him..."

"What?" said Mordred. "Give him what?"

"His, uh, gold," said Angus softly.

But Mordred never heard a word, for at that moment, a huge hunk of the entryway ceiling crashed to the floor.

"It's Herbert Dungeonstone's ghost!" cried Erica.

"See! He's going to destroy DSA!" Wiglaf shouted, ducking as stones crashed down around them.

The headmaster's face fell. "The knave!" he cried. "He's come at last."

"So it's true? You did rob them, sir?" asked Erica.

"It's no more than they tried to do to me!" cried Mordred. "All the gold they ever had came from the pockets of others. All right, maybe I *did* take their gold. But look at all the good I do with it. I turn you small, helpless lads into dragon-slaying heroes!"

"Please, Uncle!" cried Angus. "Give the ghost some of your gold so he'll go away!"

"Some?" said Mordred. "Ha! He'll want ALL my gold."

"That...that is true, sir," said Wiglaf.

"Of course it is!" snapped Mordred. "When you're greedy, some is never enough. And, to tell you the truth, ALL comes up a bit short."

"That is just what Herbert Dungeonstone said," remarked Wiglaf.

Mordred squeezed his bear and turned to Angus. "This is all your doing, nephew!"

"Me? No, Uncle!" said Angus.

"You brought that ghost here," said Mordred. "You are trying to get back at me for cutting your allowance in half!"

"But, Uncle," said Angus, "you don't give me an allowance."

"I don't?" Mordred looked puzzled. "That's odd. Your mother sends me money every... Never mind!"

"Speaking of Mother, has she sent my latest goodie box?" asked Angus eagerly.

"Goodie box!" roared Mordred. "This is no time to speak of goodies! You must arm yourselves, lads! Go forth and fight! Rid this castle of the ghost at once!"

"We cannot get rid of him, sir," said Wiglaf. "But you can."

"How?" cried Mordred. "Quick! Tell me. I will do anything. Anything!"

Wiglaf smiled. "Give him your bag of gold and he will go away."

Mordred brought his bear up to his face and bit its ear. "Give...my..." His eyes bulged dangerously. "Are you out of your mind?"

"Uncle! Quick! Look behind you!" warned Angus.

Mordred whirled around and saw a suit of

armor creeping up on him.

"Zounds!" he cried.

Now the armor's helmet floated up into the air.

"Double zounds!" cried Mordred.

The shield sprang forward. The sword quickly followed. It zigzagged in front of Mordred's face.

"Don't hurt me!" cried the headmaster. "Or my bear!"

The ghost let out a blood-chilling laugh.

The headmaster raced off down the hallway with the helmet, shield, and sword right behind him. He doubled back, and Wiglaf, Erica, and Angus flattened themselves against his office door so as not to be trampled.

"Be gone, Dungeonstone!" Mordred shouted as he ran. "Scat! Shoo! Back to your tomb, I say!"

The ghost's banging did not wake more DSA lads. But the bellowing headmaster did.

Now dozens of lads were staring down from the top of the staircase.

Mordred glanced up as he ran.

"Back...to...bed...lads," he panted. "Go...on!" On he ran, the floating armor hot on his heels.

A peal of ghostly laughter rang out.

Up on the staircase, Torblad suddenly flew into the air.

"Whoaaaaa!" he cried as he was lifted higher and higher. He grabbed the chandelier and clung to it for dear life.

Now Baldrick was whisked into the air. He soared over Wiglaf's head, then dropped to the floor.

"Owie!" cried Baldrick.

"I can't watch." Mordred shielded his eyes with his bear.

"Help! Help!" cried Torblad, still clutching the chandelier. "DSA is haunted!"

Chapter 9

"**B**lazing King Ken's britches!" cried Mordred. He turned and fled into his office.

Wiglaf, Angus, and Erica came after him.

Mordred sped through a connecting door into his bedroom. The others followed.

A gold-trimmed suit of armor stood at the head of a fancy red bed. Mordred jumped under his covers. He cradled his bear in his arms. "Everything will be all right," he whispered to his bear. "Yes, it will."

A wide-eyed Lady Lobelia rushed in. She was wearing a fuzzy yellow robe.

"Is the sky falling?" she cried. "Have the peasants revolted? What in the name of Saint George's mustache is going on out there?"

"It is Herbert Dungeonstone's ghost, Auntie," said Angus. "He is tearing down our school!"

"But why?" said Lobelia. "He helped to found DSA. Isn't that right, Mordie?"

"It's a long story, sister," Mordred said quickly. "The point is, the knave is after my gold!" He sat up in his bed. "Let us flee, Lobelia. You and me! I'll pack up my gold, and we'll hit the road!"

Lobelia folded her arms. "No," she said. "I put the good of the school before my own good. Or yours, Mordie."

"Oh, bother." Mordred sank back against his silken pillows.

"We must get rid of this ghost," said Lobelia. "I'll go get some garlic."

"That's for vampires, Auntie," said Angus.

"Ah," said Lobelia. "Then we must expose the ghost to sunlight."

"That's werewolves," said Wiglaf.

"Shall we ring bells and clang gongs?" asked Lobelia.

Erica shook her head. "Demons."

A terrible crash sounded outside the room.

Lobelia winced. "If the castle does collapse, I don't want to be caught in my robe!" She hurried off to her chamber.

"Lads," said Mordred, "you seem to know a great deal about getting rid of monsters."

"I have a book on it," Angus said.

"Tell me—how do we get rid of this blasted ghost?" asked Mordred.

Angus shook his head. "Ghosts are nearly impossible to get rid of, Uncle," he said. "Just give Dungeonstone your gold."

The loudest crash yet thundered. Mordred leaped out of bed. They all hurried from the room to see what had happened.

Wiglaf froze at the scene that met his eyes.

The entire entryway ceiling had collapsed. Students were running through the rubble to get out of the castle.

"Help! Help!" lads cried as fiery torches zoomed after them, seemingly on their own.

Ghostly laughter filled the air.

Baldrick and others were lugging their trunks down the staircase, making an escape.

Up on the landing, the big Marley brothers had armed themselves with lances.

"Which way did he go?" called Barley.

"We'll get him!" called Charlie.

"We'll whack him!" called Farley.

"We'll run him through!" called Harley.

A stream of DSA lads and teachers were running out to the castle yard.

"They're heading for the gatehouse!" cried Erica. "But the drawbridge is up!"

"There is no way out of DSA except swimming the moat," cried Wiglaf.

"Ugh!" said Angus. "It's full of eels and much scarier than any ghost."

"Come on!" said Erica. And they all ran

into the castle yard. The headmaster came, too, lugging his teddy bear.

In the moonlight, Wiglaf saw a few brave lads holding their noses and jumping into the moat.

"Where is that ghost?" bellowed Mordred. "Just let me get my hands on him!"

"Right here!" cried Dungeonstone. And he appeared, glowing against the starry sky. The red brew still sloshed around in his gut.

"Help, help! A ghost!" bawled lads and teachers alike. Many ran back into the castle.

"This is the tip of the iceberg," said the ghost of Herbert Dungeonstone. "I'll bring the whole place down unless I gets me gold!"

"Never!" cried Mordred. "Never!"

Dungeonstone flitted over to the scrubbing block and scooped up a dirty pot. He hurled it against the castle wall. BAM!

Amid the shrieks and pandemonium, a large, fully armored figure strode silently out of the DSA castle. He wore a helmet with the visor down, hiding his face.

"Who is that?" asked Wiglaf.

"Coach Plungett?" said Angus.

"No, he's by the gatehouse," said Wiglaf.

The figure carried a lance.

"I know!" said Erica. "I bet it's Harley Marley!"

The armored knight made his way down the steps, shaking his lance at the ghost.

"Oh, you wants a fight, do you?" cried Dungeonstone. "You'll be sorry!"

The ghost gave a shrill whistle and called, "Come, Daggertooth!" A wind rose, and out of the sky came a great winged dragon's ghost.

Students and teachers screamed in fear. They ducked, covering their heads.

The dragon ghost flew down and landed beside Dungeonstone, who hopped onto its back. The creature let out a terrible roar. Ghostly plumes of smoke poured from its nostrils.

The armor-clad knight advanced on the mounted Dungeonstone, waving the lance.

"That's the way, Harley!" cried Erica.

"Get him, Harley!" cried Angus.

Wiglaf was speechless. He had never seen anyone so brave as Harley Marley.

Daggertooth spread his wings and took off. He swooped down so that Dungeonstone could take a whack at the knight with his sword.

Harley dodged the first blow but not the next.

The sword crashed down on the knight's helmet. He sank to the ground.

The dragon ghost slowly circled above, and Dungeonstone laughed. "Anyone else want to fight?" he cried.

"No! No!" cried the students.

"Yes!" cried Mordred. "Go on, pupils! Fight him! Drive him away!"

Wiglaf, Angus, and Erica ignored Mordred

and ran to the fallen knight.

"Help me get his helmet off," said Erica. Angus and Wiglaf took hold of the helmet, too. They pulled and wiggled and at last it popped off.

"Egad!" cried Angus.

"Zounds!" cried Erica.

Wiglaf stared in awe. The brave student wasn't Harley Marley, after all. Wiglaf was staring down at the face of Janice Smotherbottom. Her lips curved up in a strange smile. Her eyes were shut.

She was out cold.

Chapter 10

"Janice is very brave!" said Wiglaf.

"And very knocked-out," said Erica. "Look at that bump on her head. Let's get her into the castle."

The three picked her up.

"She's very heavy," said Angus as they struggled up the steps and into the castle.

They carried Janice into Mordred's bedroom. Wiglaf took the wad of green gum from her mouth and stuck it on Mordred's bedpost.

"Uncle Mordred won't mind," said Angus.

"No," said Wiglaf, fanning Janice. "After all, she was trying to get rid of the ghost."

Erica sighed. "Janice won't want to stay at

DSA now. And I can't blame her."

Wiglaf said, "Maybe we should summon Zelnoc. Maybe he can get rid of the ghost."

"But Zelnoc is the world's worst wizard," said Erica.

Wiglaf shrugged. "What else can we do?"

Another crash sounded in the castle yard. Angus ran outside to see what was going on. He ran back, panting for breath.

"The castle yard is a wreck!" he said. "Dungeonstone's ghost has smashed our practice dragon to bits. Now he's headed for the jousting scarecrow."

Wiglaf wasted no time. He chanted the wizard's name backwards three times: "Conlez, Conlez, Conlez!"

Mordred's bedroom quickly filled with purple smoke.

As it cleared, Wiglaf made out a thin, white-bearded man wearing a pointed cap. A large black bird sat on his left shoulder.

"Zelnoc!" said Wiglaf.

"Wiglip?" The wizard waved away the remaining smoke. "Ah, there you are. Have you met my familiar?" He nodded toward the crow. "This is George, my new helper in all things magical. Well, what'll it be this time, Waglaf? George will help me grant your every wish. Won't you, George?"

The wizard reached up to stroke George. But the creature pecked his hand.

"Ow!" Zelnoc cried. "You nasty nipper!"

George began grooming his feathers.

"Excuse me, sir," said Wiglaf. "We need help. A ghost is trying to destroy our school."

George suddenly spread his wings. He flew over and perched on the helmet of a suit of armor. He began picking at the gold trim.

"Warts and toadstools!" exclaimed the wizard. "George isn't bonding with me like *The Wizard Handbook* said he would."

"Can you get rid of the ghost, Zelnoc?"

asked Erica. "Before he brings down the whole school?"

Zelnoc drummed his fingers on his cheek. "Ever play Rock, Dagger, Parchment?" he asked. "You know. Rock." The wizard made a fist. "Dagger." He stuck out his pointer finger. "Parchment." He flattened out his hand. "Rock smashes Dagger, Dagger cuts Parchment, Parchment covers Rock."

"We know how to play the game," said Wiglaf. "But we don't know how to get rid of this ghost."

"That's what I'm getting at," said Zelnoc. "You see, wizards can get rid of witches. Witches can get rid of ghouls. Ghouls can get rid of bats. Bats can get rid of bugs. Bugs can get rid of damsels. Damsels can get rid of trolls. Trolls can—"

"Stop!" cried Erica. "Does this have anything to do with ghosts?"

Zelnoc looked thoughtful. "I'm not sure it

does," he said. "Except to say that there's no other monster, demon, etc. that can get rid of a ghost."

"Isn't there any way you can help us, wizard?" asked Wiglaf.

"I could chant the general ghost-be-gone spell," Zelnoc said. "It's never worked for me. But there's always a first time. George? How about some help?"

The crow ignored Zelnoc and continued to groom its glossy feathers.

"All right, here goes." The wizard closed his eyes and chanted:

> "Protoplasmic spirit who
> Walks through walls and shouts out BOO,
> Phantom zombie pale and wan,
> Ghost! I say to you, BE GONE!"

A flash of lightning lit the early morning sky. Wiglaf felt the room grow cold.

"Oops!" said Zelnoc.

The room grew colder still.

"What do you mean, oops?" said Erica.

"I think I'll be going now," said Zelnoc. "Come, George!"

The crow began screeching and cawing.

"Wait, wizard!" cried Wiglaf.

But purple smoke was already filling the air. Wiglaf could not see a thing.

Erica's voice carried over George's caws: "I knew this was a bad idea!"

At last, the smoke faded. Zelnoc and his crow were gone.

But Wiglaf's eyes grew wide. For in the wizard's place stood another ghostly knight!

"Sir—Sir Ichabod Popquiz?" asked Wiglaf.

Did they now have two robber ghosts loose in their school?

Angus pointed to the ghost. "I know you!" he cried. "You're Sir Jeffrey Scabpicker!"

Chapter 11

"Zee name," said the ghost, floating toward them, "ees French. You say like thees: scah-peek-AY. You try eet."

"Scah-peek-AY," murmured the three.

"Bon!" The ghost kissed the tips of his fingers. "Now tell me, why haf I been called from my peaceful eternal rest?"

"Sir Jeffrey was married to Auntie Lobelia," Angus told the others before bowing politely to the new ghost. "We need help, sir," he said, "to get rid of Herbert Dungeonstone's ghost. He's wrecking our school."

"The fiend!" cried Sir Jeffrey. He drew his sword. "I shall right thees wrong! I shall send heem back to hees grave! But first, I must see my lovely Lady Lobelia."

"Couldn't you see her after you get rid of the ghost, Sir Jeffrey?" asked Angus. "He's really doing a job on this old castle."

"No, no, no." Sir Jeffrey wagged a finger at them. "That weel never do. A proper knight must be sent into battle by a fair damsel. Lady Lobelia weel geev to me a love token. A perfumed hankie, perhaps. Or one of her hair ribbons. Thees token I weell tuck into my armor, next to my heart. Then, and only then, weel I go into battle!"

"All right," said Angus. "Let's go."

"Wait," said Wiglaf. "Sir Jeffrey, if the other students see you..."

"Ah, I weel frighten them, no? How ees thees?" Sir Jeffrey vanished.

"Janice will be safe here," said Wiglaf.

The three pupils and the invisible ghost left the headmaster's bedroom. They made their way through falling stones and flying armor to

Lady Lobelia's door.

Angus knocked. "We must be ready to catch her if she faints," he told his friends.

Lady Lobelia opened the door.

Just then, Sir Jeffrey reappeared.

"Oh, my stars!" Lobelia cried. "Can it really be you?"

"Darling Lobelia!" said Sir Jeffrey. "I weesh you could throw your arms around me. But alas! You would embrace only air."

"Jeffrey! It *is* you!" cried Lobelia. "And still wearing the armor I picked out for your burial. Come in! Come in!"

"Sir Jeffrey is going to get rid of Herbert Dungeonstone for us, Auntie," said Angus.

"Still the perfect knight, eh, Jeffrey?" said Lobelia. "That armor fits you like a glove. Turn around. Let me see it from all sides."

Sir Jeffrey happily turned.

"Did you ever see a more perfect knight?" asked Lobelia. "Even as a ghost, you're a spiffy

dresser, Jeffrey."

Sir Jeffrey smiled. "Let me recite some love poems to you, lovely Lobelia."

"But, sir!" said Wiglaf. "What about Herbert Dungeonstone?"

Sir Jeffrey frowned. "Do you theenk he would like to hear a love poem?"

"I mean, what about getting rid of him?" said Wiglaf.

"A knight who has not recited a love poem to hees damsel can never triumph in battle!" declared Sir Jeffrey. He cleared his throat.

"My love for you ees like a cheese,
A cheese that I would like to squeeze.
My love for you ees like green peas.
Tell me that you like peas, please!
My love for you ees like a sneeze,
Floating on a gentle breeze.
My love for you..."

"Oh, Jeffrey!" crooned Lobelia when at last

he had finished his poem. "That was beautiful!"

"Here ees another!" said Sir Jeffrey.

A crash sounded above their heads.

"That came from the dining hall!" cried Angus, alarmed. "Sir Jeffrey, we have to hurry, please!"

"One more, my sweet," said Lobelia, never taking her eyes from Sir Jeffrey.

Sir Jeffrey smiled and began to recite a poem about Lobelia being his bunny wunny wabbit and his fuzzy little ducky wucky.

"Yuck!" said Erica. "Come on! We'll deal with this ourselves!"

Angus, Wiglaf, and Erica ran up to the dining hall. They stopped under the arch.

In the early dawn light, they saw that the place was under attack! Soup bowls were flying overhead. Ladles, too. The students were cowering under the tables.

"Take that, ghost, wherever you are!" cried Frypot as he ran around the dining hall swatting

at thin air with a frying pan.

Dungeonstone only giggled. Then the invisible ghost lifted up Frypot's cauldron of eel chowder.

"Look out!" cried Wiglaf. The cauldron tilted and eel chowder rained down upon everyone in the dining hall.

"Stop! Stop!" cried the lads.

"Stop?" said Herbert Dungeonstone. He appeared suddenly, standing on the head table. "I'll stop as soon as Mordred hands over the gold!"

Just then, Lobelia and Sir Jeffrey appeared in the entryway.

"*Zut!*" said Sir Jeffrey. He drew his sword. "Weecked Dungeonstone! Prepare to die—again!"

Chapter 12

Herbert Dungeonstone floated swiftly over to Sir Jeffrey Scabpicker. The two drew their swords.

Wiglaf, Angus, Erica, and Lobelia ran behind an overturned table to watch.

"Go, Sir Jeffrey!" called Erica.

Dungeonstone grabbed his sword with both hands. He swung it at Sir Jeffrey's head. In the nick of time, Sir Jeffrey ducked.

But he was no match for Sir Herbert. Wiglaf saw that, with each blow, Sir Jeffrey was growing weaker, paler. Wiglaf had to do something to help!

"Hey, look, Dungeonstone!" he called. "Here's Mordred with the gold!"

"What? Where?" Dungeonstone swiveled his head around.

Sir Jeffrey wasted no time. He pulled back his sword and ran Dungeonstone through.

"You are beaten, varlet!" cried Sir Jeffrey.

"Yay, Jeffie!" cried Lobelia. "My hero!"

Dungeonstone only smirked. He easily yanked out Sir Jeffrey's sword. The red brew spurted out of the hole in his ghostly gut and onto the floor.

"Aww!" said Dungeonstone, wagging Sir Jeffrey's sword in the old knight's face. "You lost your weapon!" He began slashing at Sir Jeffrey with both swords.

Sir Jeffrey dodged the blades as he floated ever nearer to Frypot's cauldron. He lifted it up, but Dungeonstone grabbed the huge pot from him. He dumped what was left of the eel chowder onto Sir Jeffrey's head.

"Oh, that chowder will ruin his armor," said Lobelia.

Sir Jeffrey snatched back his sword and ran Dungeonstone through again. If the two had not been ghosts, each would have died many times over. But they *were* ghosts, so the fight went on and on.

"Is it just me," Angus said, "or is Sir Jeffrey getting hard to see?"

Wiglaf looked. Indeed, the noble knight seemed to be fading.

"Zelnoc's spell must be wearing off!" said Erica. "Ooooh, that lousy wizard!"

Sir Jeffrey did some fancy footwork. He caught Dungeonstone by surprise and knocked his sword out of his hand. Sir Jeffrey put the tip of his sword to Dungeonstone's Adam's apple.

"You weel leave Dragon Slayers' Academy!" whispered the good ghost knight. "And you weel never come back!"

Wiglaf could hardly hear Sir Jeffrey. His voice was fading along with the rest of him.

"I'm not leaving!" cried Dungeonstone. "You are! Look at you!"

Sir Jeffrey looked down at his ghostly self.

"*Zut!*" he squeaked. He glanced over at Lobelia. "Adieu, my lovely! Parting ees such sweet sorrow. Adieuuuuuuuuuu..."

"Oh, Jeffrey, don't go!" cried Lobelia.

But Sir Jeffrey was already gone.

Dungeonstone wasted no time. He began overturning more dining tables. He threw the benches against the wall.

"Stop!" cried Wiglaf.

"Stop!" cried Angus.

"STOP!" cried Mordred, sweeping into the dining hall. His violet eyes widened as they took in the terrible mess.

Dungeonstone floated over to Mordred.

The two stared at each other.

"So we meet again," said Dungeonstone. "Are you ready to hand over me gold?"

"Yesssss," said Mordred, his violet eyes

gleaming. "I shall give it to you—all of it. Come!"

Mordred turned and left the dining hall. Dungeonstone whooshed out after him.

"I can't believe my ears," said Erica.

"Our school is saved!" cried Wiglaf.

"Uncle Mordred would never give up so easily," said Angus. "He must have something up his sleeve."

"Let us follow them," said Erica. "Come on!"

Chapter 13

Wiglaf, Erica, Angus, and Lobelia ran to the back of the dining hall. Angus opened a door. He led the way down back stairs and through narrow passageways to another door. Angus pushed it open, and they stepped into Mordred's bedroom.

Janice was still passed out on the bed.

"Listen!" said Erica. "Do you hear that?"

Wiglaf hoped it wasn't more moaning. He listened. And he heard voices coming from Mordred's office next door.

All four of them crept closer to the door to hear more.

"You win, Dungeonstone," Mordred was saying. "I'll give you my gold."

"I can smell it," said Dungeonstone's ghost. "Hand it over. Be quick about it!"

"Fine, fine," said Mordred. "I'll give you every last golden coin!"

Angus turned to Lobelia.

"I can't believe what I'm hearing," he whispered.

"He must have some trick in mind," Lobelia answered. "But what?"

She placed a hand on the doorknob and turned it slowly. She cracked the door open. The four pressed close to see.

Wiglaf saw Mordred, his teddy bear still stashed under one arm, lift up a large red-and-white striped box.

Angus gasped.

From the box, Mordred lifted a bulging net bag filled with gold coins.

"No!" Angus breathed.

"Me gold!" cried Dungeonstone. He hugged it to his chest. "At last I have me gold.

Now I can return to me grave and rest, like Icky's doing."

Wiglaf smiled. Any minute now, Dungeonstone's greedy ghost would leave DSA once and for all time!

But suddenly, Angus flung the door open.

What was going on? Wiglaf wondered.

Angus stomped into Mordred's office.

"Nephew!" cried the startled headmaster. "Away! Leave me be!"

"That bag isn't yours to give away, Uncle Mordred!" Angus shouted. "It's from my goodie box!"

"Huh?" said the ghost.

Angus turned to the ghost. "Those aren't gold coins!" he cried. "They're chocolate! And they're *mine*!"

"Don't listen to him!" cried Mordred. He began whacking Angus with his teddy bear. "He's a liar! Be gone, nephew! Before I put you in the thumbscrews!"

Angus ran to his aunt Lobelia to escape being whacked.

Meanwhile, Dungeonstone's ghost was fumbling with a gold coin. Wiglaf saw that he'd succeeded in peeling back the gold foil.

"He's right!" roared the ghost, flinging the bag to the floor. "It's bloody chocolate!"

"I knew it!" called Angus. "Ever since the DSA team won that trophy full of chocolate coins at the all-schools brainpower tournament, Mother's been putting chocolate coins in my goodie box."

The ghost sniffed loudly. "But I know me gold's here, too. I can smell it! Now, all I have to do is find it!" The ghost began searching the office.

Wiglaf saw an odd smile creep onto the headmaster's lips.

"Nonny, nonny, nonny!" chanted Mordred. "You can't find my money!" He began skipping around the room with his bear.

"Oh, my," said Lobelia. "He's gone dotty."

The DSA trophy case came crashing down.

Mordred's robe billowed out behind him as he skipped. He sang, "Nonny nonny toot toot toot! You will never find my loot!"

As the headmaster sang, the ghost sniffed. He drew closer and closer to Mordred until his pointed snout was only inches away.

"I think I know where me gold is hidden," the ghost said, and he lunged for Mordred's teddy bear.

"What! How did you guess!" cried Mordred. He whisked the bear away from the ghost and clutched it tightly to his chest. "My gold," he murmured. "Mine! It took me months of scheming to lure Janice away from Dragon Whackers. I earned this gold and I'm not giving it away."

"Rubble!" cried Herbert Dungeonstone. "That's all that will be left of this school. Rubble!"

The ghost grabbed the bear. Mordred clung to it tightly. It was tug-of-war! But the ghost was quickly out-tugged.

"Sir!" cried Erica. "If we have no school, how will we learn to become dragon slayers?"

"Take a correspondence course," growled Mordred, never taking his eyes from the ghost.

"Sir!" cried Wiglaf. "We can get you more gold."

Mordred tilted his head. "You can?"

"Oh, yes, sir," said Wiglaf. "The world is full of gold."

"Full of gold," Mordred repeated dreamily.

"Lots of gold!" cried Wiglaf. "Bags of it!"

"Let me take this one small bear from you, Uncle," said Angus.

"Yes, let 'im!" said Dungeonstone.

"All...all right," said Mordred. "Take it."

Angus reached for the bear. But Mordred kept it hugged firmly to his chest.

"I need some help," said Angus.

"I know!" said Wiglaf. "The Duke of Doublechin torture! It worked in the Cave of Doom."

"Forgive us, sir," said Erica.

With that, Angus, Wiglaf, and Erica pounced on Mordred and began tickling. "Whoo-hoo-hoo!" cried Mordred. "Stop!"

But they kept on, tickling his tummy, under his chin, even his armpits.

"Ho ho! Have mercy!" cried Mordred.

"Let go, Mordie!" said Lobelia. She began tickling him, too.

Wiglaf pulled off Mordred's boots and tickled his feet.

"Whooo!" cried Mordred. And at last his gold-ringed fingers let go of the bear.

"Got it!" cried Lobelia, holding up the bear in one hand.

"No, no," Mordred whimpered. Tears ran down his cheeks.

"Me gold!" cried Dungeonstone. He

swooped over and snatched the bear out of Lobelia's hands. He shook it. Inside, it jingled. "Now I have robbed the robber that robbed us robbers! Now I can rest forever peaceful in me tomb!"

"Excuse me, sir," said Wiglaf. "What will you do with the gold?"

"Do?" Dungeonstone shrugged. "I only wanted what was mine. Fair's fair, even if I was a highwayman and robber. As a ghost, I have no use for gold. On me way back to me grave, I'll dump the gold into the sea."

"Into the..." Mordred began. THUNK!

He fell to the ground in a faint.

"Farewell! Farewell!" cried the greedy ghost. Then Herbert Dungeonstone vanished, but his laughter echoed throughout DSA long after he was gone.

Chapter 14

"Ohhhh!" A groan sounded.

"It's Janice!" said Erica. "She's coming to!"

The three ran into Mordred's bedroom.

"Janice?" said Wiglaf. "Are you all right?"

Janice sat up. She rubbed the bump on her head. "This is nothing," she said. "I've gotten far worse knocks jousting."

"Do you want help packing?" Erica asked.

Janice frowned. "Packing?"

"I know you will not stay at DSA," said Erica.

"Not after all that's happened," added Wiglaf.

"Are you joking, lads?" said Janice. "My old school was boring compared to this."

"Yay!" said Wiglaf.

"That's reason to celebrate," said Angus.

"Let's go back to the dorm room. Can you walk, Janice?" asked Erica.

"Walk?" said Janice, springing out of bed. "I'll race you to the dorm!"

Janice won.

Angus came in last, for he was carrying his large goodie box. Back in the dorm room, he shouted, "Stash for everyone!"

"Is DSA always this exciting?" asked Janice. She had parked her gum behind her ear and was munching on a gold chocolate coin.

"Sort of," Wiglaf told her.

"So what's up next, guys?" asked Janice.

Erica leaned forward and whispered a secret into Janice's ear.

"You *are?*" said Janice. "All right!"

Erica grinned. "Now, I have a job for the four of us." Keeping her voice low, she said, "We shall wait until everyone is asleep. Then we shall sneak down to the tool shop and get hammers and chisels..."

"Welcome to Founders Day breakfast!" called Lady Lobelia as the students straggled into the dining hall late that morning. "Come in, pupils. Have a bite to eat before the Founders Day Clean-up-the-Castle Relay Game begins!"

Once more, a black cloth had been draped over the school sign. But this time, Wiglaf did not wonder why. He knew.

Mordred sat at the headmaster's table. His violet eyes were bright red from crying.

When everyone was seated, Erica popped up. "Mordred, sir!" she said. "I have a Founders Day surprise for you."

Mordred only blew his nose: HONK!

"Janice Smotherbottom," Erica went on, "is not the first lass at DSA."

Mordred blinked. He waved his hankie at her to go on.

Erica whipped off her DSA helmet, and two long braids of brown hair fell down her back.

Gasps sounded throughout the dining hall.

"I, sir, am not Eric," said Erica. "I am Erica von Royale. A lass."

Janice and Wiglaf ran over to the black-cloth draped sign. They yanked on the cloth, and down it fell. Now the sign read:

DRAGON SLAYERS' ACADEMY FOR LADS AND LASSES.

Mordred still looked stunned. Then he suddenly leaped up.

"YES!" he shouted. "DSA for Lads and Lasses! I'll admit girls to DSA. Lots of girls! Double the students! Double the tuition! Oh, why didn't I think of this years ago? It's brilliant! I am going to make a bloody fortune!" He grinned out at his students. "Frypot!" he shouted. "Don't serve that week-old eel, after

all. Break out the cheese and sausages!"

The room grew still. You could have heard a pin drop.

Frypot stuck his head out of the kitchen. "Are you feeling all right, sir?"

"It's Founders Day, Frypot!" cried Mordred. "Bring it, I say. All of it! And pop open a jug of cider." He grinned. "Double the tuition! Oh, we have much to celebrate!"

Wiglaf, Angus, Erica, and Janice Smotherbottom clinked their cider cups together and shouted, "Let's hear it for DSA!"

THE END

~DSA~
YEARBOOK

Goldius est goodius!

The Campus of Dragon Slayers' Academy

DSA

Lady Lobelia's Chamber

Dr. Pluck's Science Lab

Tun Exit

Mordred's Classroom

Headmaster's Office

Sta

Cas Ya

Dining Hall

To Dungeon

Scrubbing Class

Prac Dra

Yorick's Quick Change-O-Rama Camp site

~Our Founders~

Sir Herbert Dungeonstone

Sir Ichabod Popquiz

～ Our Philosophy ～

Sir Herbert and Sir Ichabod founded
Dragon Slayers' Academy on a simple
principle still held dear today: Any lad—
no matter how weak, yellow-bellied, lazy,
pigeon-toed, smelly, or unwilling—can be
transformed into a fearless dragon slayer
who goes for the gold. After four years
at DSA, lads will finally be of some worth
to their parents, as well as a source of
great wealth to this distinguished
academy.* ** ***

* Please note that Dragon Slayers' Academy is a strictly-for-profit
institution.

** Dragon Slayers' Academy reserves the right to keep some of the gold
and treasure that any student recovers from a dragon's lair.

*** The exact amount of treasure given to a student's family is determined
solely by our esteemed headmaster, Mordred. The amount shall be no less
than 1/500th of the treasure and no greater than 1/499th.

Mordred de Marvelous

Mordred graduated from Dragon Bludgeon High, second in his class. The other student, Lionel Flyzwattar, went on to become headmaster of Dragon Stabbers' Prep. Mordred spent years as part-time, semi-substitute student teacher at Dragon Whackers' Alternative School, all the while pursuing his passion for mud wrestling. Inspired by how filthy rich Flyzwattar had become by running a school, Mordred founded Dragon Slayers' Academy in CMLXXIV, and has served as headmaster ever since.

Known to the Boys as: Mordred de Miser
Dream: Piles and piles of dragon gold
Reality: Yet to see a single gold coin
Best-Kept Secret: Mud wrestled under the name Macho-Man Mordie
Plans for the Future: Will retire to the Bahamas . . . as soon as he gets his hands on a hoard

Lady Lobelia

Lobelia de Marvelous is Mordred's sister and a graduate of the exclusive If-You-Can-Read-This-You-Can-Design-Clothes Fashion School. Lobelia has offered fashion advice to the likes of King Felix the Husky and Eric the Terrible Dresser. In CMLXXIX, Lobelia married the oldest living knight, Sir Jeffrey Scabpicker III. That's when she gained the title of Lady Lobelia, but—alas!—only a very small fortune, which she wiped out in a single wild shopping spree. Lady Lobelia has graced Dragon Slayers' Academy with many visits, and can be heard around campus saying, "Just because I live in the Middle Ages doesn't mean I have to look middle-aged."

Known to the Boys as: Lady Lo Lo
Dream: Frightfully fashionable
Reality: Frightful
Best-Kept Secret: Shops at Dark-Age Discount Dress Dungeon
Plans for the Future: New uniforms for the boys with mesh tights and lace tunics

Sir Mort du Mort

Sir Mort is our well-loved professor of Dragon Slaying for Beginners as well as Intermediate and Advanced Dragon Slaying. Sir Mort says that, in his youth, he was known as the Scourge of Dragons. (We're not sure what it means, but it sounds scary.) His last encounter was with the most dangerous dragon of them all: Knight-shredder. Early in the battle, Sir Mort took a nasty blow to his helmet and has never been the same since.

Known to the Boys as: The Old Geezer
Dream: Outstanding Dragon Slayer
Reality: Just plain out of it
Best-Kept Secret: He can't remember
Plans for the Future: Taking a little nap

～ Faculty ～

Coach Wendell Plungett

Coach Plungett spent many years questing in the Dark Forest before joining the Athletic Department at DSA. When at last he strode out of the forest, leaving his dragon-slaying days behind him, Coach Plungett was the most muscle-bulging, physically fit, manliest man to be found anywhere north of Nowhere Swamp. "I am what you call a hunk," the coach admits. At DSA, Plungett wears a number of hats—or, helmets. Besides PE Teacher, he is Slaying Coach, Square-Dance Director, Pep-Squad Sponsor, and Privy Inspector. He hopes to meet a damsel—she needn't be in distress—with whom he can share his love of heavy metal music and long dinners by candlelight.

Known to the Boys as: Coach
Dream: Tough as nails
Reality: Sleeps with a stuffed dragon named Foofoo
Best-Kept Secret: Just pull his hair
Plans for the Future: Finding his lost lady love

Brother Dave

Brother Dave is the DSA librarian. He belongs to the Little Brothers of the Peanut Brittle, an order known for doing impossibly good deeds and cooking up endless batches of sweet peanut candy. How exactly did Brother Dave wind up at Dragon Slayers' Academy? After a batch of his extra-crunchy peanut brittle left three children from Toenail toothless, Brother Dave vowed to do a truly impossible good deed. Thus did he offer to be librarian at a school world-famous for considering reading and writing a complete and utter waste of time. Brother Dave hopes to change all that.

⚜

Known to the Boys as: Bro Dave
Dream: Boys reading in the libary
Reality: Boys sleeping in the library
Best-Kept Secret: Uses Cliff's Notes
Plans for the Future: Copying out all the lyrics to "Found a Peanut" for the boys

~ Faculty ~

Professor Prissius Pluck

Professor Pluck graduated from Peter Piper Picked a Peck of Pickled Peppers Prep, and went on to become a professor of Science at Dragon Slayers' Academy. His specialty is the Multiple Choice Pop Test. The boys who take Dragon Science, Professor Pluck's popular class,

- **a)** are amazed at the great quantities of saliva Professor P. can project
- **b)** try never to sit in the front row
- **c)** beg Headmaster Mordred to transfer them to another class
- **d)** all of the above

Known to the Boys as: Old Spit Face
Dream: Proper pronunciation of *p*'s
Reality: Let us spray
Best-Kept Secret: Has never seen a pippi-hippo-pappa-peepus up close
Plans for the Future: Is working on a cure for chapped lips

Frypot

How Frypot came to be the cook at DSA is something of a mystery. Rumors abound. Some say that when Mordred bought the broken-down castle for his school, Frypot was already in the kitchen and he simply stayed on. Others say that Lady Lobelia hired Frypot because he was so speedy at washing dishes. Still others say Frypot knows many a dark secret that keeps him from losing his job. But no one ever, *ever* says that Frypot was hired because of his excellent cooking skills.

Known to the Boys as: Who needs a nickname with a real name like Frypot?
Dream: Cleaner kitchen
Reality: Kitchen cleaner
Best-Kept Secret: Takes long bubble baths in the moat
Plans for the Future: Has signed up for a beginning cooking class

~Staff~

Yorick

Yorick is Chief Scout at DSA. His knack for masquerading as almost anything comes from his years with the Merry Minstrels and Dancing Damsels Players, where he won an award for his role as the Glass Slipper in *Cinderella*. However, when he was passed over for the part of Mama Bear in *Goldilocks*, Yorick decided to seek a new way of life. He snuck off in the night and, by dawn, still dressed in the bear suit, found himself walking up Huntsmans Path. Mordred spied him from a castle window, recognized his talent for disguise, and hired him as Chief Scout on the spot.

Known to the Boys as: Who's that?
Dream: Master of Disguise
Reality: Mordred's Errand Boy
Best-Kept Secret: Likes dressing up as King Ken
Plans for the Future: To lose the bunny suit

～ Students ～

Wiglaf of Pinwick

Wiglaf, our newest lad, hails from a hovel outside the village of Pinwick, which makes Toenail look like a thriving metropolis. Being one of thirteen children, Wiglaf had a taste of dorm life before coming to DSA and he fit right in. He started the year off with a bang when he took a stab at Coach Plungett's brown pageboy wig. Way to go, Wiggie! We hope to see more of this lad's wacky humor in the years to come.

Dream: Bold Dragon-Slaying Hero
Reality: Still hangs on to a "security" rag
Extracurricular Activities: Animal-Lovers Club, President; No More Eel for Lunch Club, President; Frypot's Scrub Team, Brush Wielder; Pig Appreciation Club, Founder
Favorite Subject: Library
Oft-Heard Saying: *"Ello-hay, Aisy-day!"*
Plans for the Future: To go for the gold!

Angus du Pangus

The nephew of Mordred and Lady Lobelia, Angus walks the line between saying, "I'm just one of the lads" and "I'm going to tell my uncle!" Will this Class I lad ever become a mighty dragon slayer? Or will he take over the kitchen from Frypot some day? We of the DSA Yearbook staff are betting on choice #2. And hey, Angus? The sooner the better!

Dream: A wider menu selection at DSA
Reality: Eel, Eel, Eel!
Extracurricular Activities: DSA Cooking Club, President; Smilin' Hal's Off-Campus Eatery, Sales Representative
Favorite Subject: Lunch
Oft-Heard Saying: *"I'm still hungry"*
Plans for the Future: To write *101 Ways to Cook a Dragon*

Erica von Royale

Now that DSA is coed, Erica is thrilled she can stop pretending to be "Eric." This peppy lass is not only a girl, she's smart, brave, loyal—and royal! Yes, that's right. It's *Princess* Erica, if you please, the daughter of King Ken and Queen Barb. It's for sure that as soon as she graduates, Erica will be slaying dragons in her home kingdom. For now only one question remains. Doesn't Erica's arm ever get tired from raising her hand so often?

Dream: Valiant Dragon Slayer
Reality: Teacher's Pet
Extracurricular Activities: Sir Lancelot Fan Club; Armor Polishing Club; Future Dragon Slayer of the Month Club; DSA Pep Squad, Founder and Cheer Composer
Favorite Subject: All of Them!!!!!
Oft-Heard Saying: *"When I am a mighty Dragon Slayer . . ."*
Plans for the Future: To take over DSA

～ Students ～

Janice Smotherbottom

Janice is a big, fun-loving party lass, and a great athlete who transferred from Dragon Whackers Alternative School. After her daddy made a bundle selling swamp land, he became a lord and began to hope that his only daughter might move up in the world. Not long after, Mordred recruited her to go to Dragon Slayers' Academy, and Lord and Lady Smotherbottom knew that Janice was on her way.

Dream: DSA Jousting Team Captain
Reality: There is no jousting team
Extracurricular Activities: DSA Party Planning Committee; Smilin' Hal's Off-Campus Eatery Club President; DSA Jousting Team, Founding Member
Favorite Subject: Gym
Oft-Heard Saying: *"Anybody got any gum?"*
Plans for the Future: To spend some of Daddy's gold coins

~ Advertisements ~